Henry Holt and Company • New York

The Little Christmas Soldier

THIERRY DEDIEU

Translated from the French by George Wen

to Serge

This is the story
of a little soldier who, one day,
proved that he was made of more than just wood.

Once upon a time, in a lopsided attic, there lived a wooden soldier. Day and night he stood guard over the other toys, looking neither right nor left, speaking not a word.

But every year, on Christmas Eve,
he broke his silence.

"Listen to me!" he cried out to the
other toys. "I shall tell you the story
of how, one Christmas Eve long ago,
I lost my legs, and almost lost my life!"

"I was born in the far, far North," he began, "where the weather was always cruel, and the wolves played hide-and-seek outside the door."

He told them of his first winter, a Christmas so bitter that even the mercury in the thermometer was frozen solid.

He told them about hands that were idle and numb, toes that were frozen stiff, chapped noses that dripped like faucets. "There's been nothing like it, before or since," he said. "Stones split wide open, icicles like pointed daggers, the only comfort the sight of beds piled high with patchwork quilts."

He told them how the wind flew under the door
and slapped the shutters, *bang, bang, bang*.
The cold broke in like a burglar, and robbed the
house of all warmth. "It seemed as if the world
was ending," he whispered, and the toys shivered.

The family he belonged to lived deep in a valley.
They had kept from freezing that winter by
burning whatever wood they had. Their only
means of warmth was a big log fire, which
had to be tended day and night.

Indeed, that very morning the family had
sacrificed their Christmas tree to the fire.
Now it was Christmas Eve, and there was
no more wood to burn.

But Christmas Eve is the night for toys.
"I was in my box," said the little soldier,
"wrapped snug and warm in cotton,
awaiting my most glorious hour."

In the fireplace, the last log was disappearing. There would be no visions of sugarplums for the children this night before Christmas: it was simply too cold to dream.

Little by little, a cruel chill crept into the room:
the milk in the cat's bowl turned into a tiny
frozen lake, a leftover turkey leg on the table
became a popsicle, an old black fly tumbled
from a frost-bitten loaf of bread and landed
plunk on a piece of fruitcake (though that
was never noticed).

"It was then that I climbed out of my box,"
said the little soldier.
"The clock was striking midnight.
I saw what I had to do."
He marched straight to the fire.

Proud and determined, the little soldier lay down
on the bed of ashes to rekindle the flame.
He stayed there till dawn, his face so radiant
it would have warmed any heart just to see it.
"You were the unknown soldier," whispered
one of the toys, and the soldier nodded.

It has been said that on that night the
twisting smoke from the family's chimney
gave rise to strange apparitions. But then,
people tell a lot of tall tales on Christmas Eve.

In the morning, when the family awoke,
their house was snug and warm.
"My body ached, and my wooden legs
were gone," said the Little Christmas Soldier.
"But the fire could not burn up my heart."

With that the story ended, and, without another word,
the little soldier returned to his place on guard
as the first rays of dawn broke on Christmas Day.

Copyright © 1992 by Albin Michel Jeunesse
Translation copyright © 1993 by Henry Holt and Company, Inc.
All rights reserved, including the right to reproduce this book or portions thereof in any form.
First American edition. Published by Henry Holt and Company, Inc., 115 West 18th Street, New York, New York 10011.
Published simultaneously in Canada by Fitzhenry & Whiteside Ltd., 91 Granton Drive, Richmond Hill, Ontario L4B 2N5.
Originally published in France by Albin Michel Jeunesse, Paris.

Library of Congress Cataloging-in-Publication Data
Dedieu, Thierry.   [Petit soldat Noël.   English]   The little Christmas soldier / Thierry Dedieu.
Summary: On Christmas Eve, a wooden soldier tells the other toys how, years ago
during a very cold winter, he sacrificed his legs to keep his family warm.
ISBN 0-8050-2612-6 (alk. paper)
[1. Christmas—Fiction.   2. Toys—Fiction.]   I. Title
PZ7.D35865Li   1993   [E]—dc20   92-40172

Printed in France
1 3 5 7 9 10 8 6 4 2